For Michele and Leon,
thank you both.

First published in Great Britain in 2003
by Piccadilly Press Ltd.,
5 Castle Road, London NW1 8PR

Text and illustration copyright
© Dana Kubick, 2003

Cover designed by Fielding Design Ltd

Printed in Hong Kong

ISBN:1 85340 619 8 (hardback)
1 85340 614 7 (paperback)

1 3 5 7 9 10 8 6 4 2

A catalogue record of this book is available
from the British Libary

After completing her BA,
Dana Kubick studied in the School of
Visual Arts in New York.
She has illustrated twelve
books, and also designs in
many different materials.
She lives in London with
her partner and two cats.

Piccadilly Press also publish:
Cats, Cats and More Cats
1 85340 605 8
(paperback)

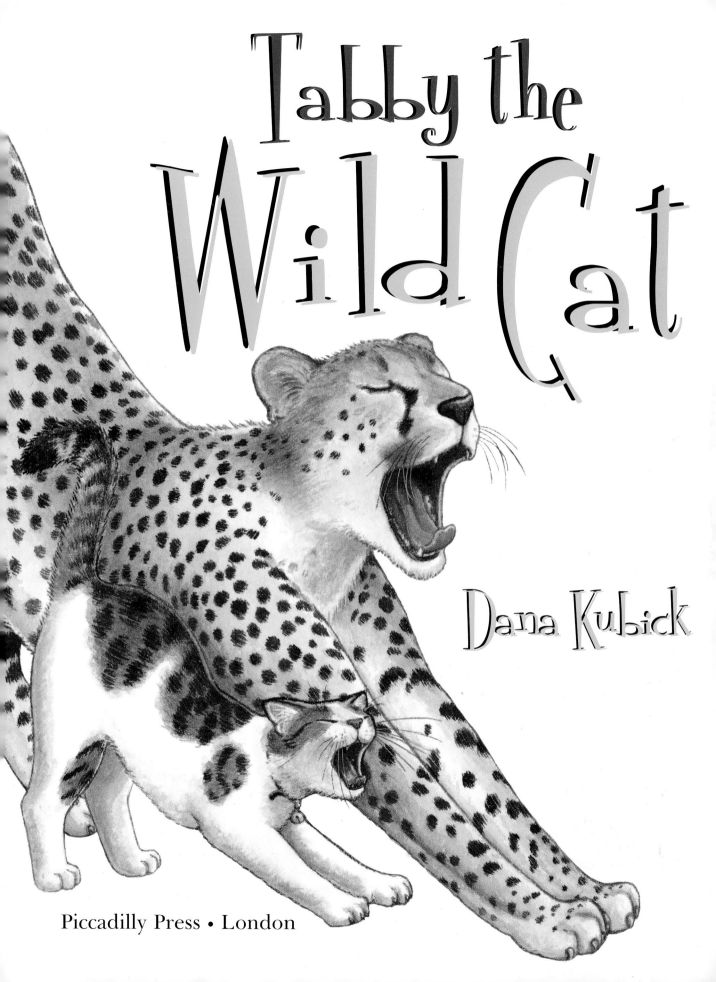

Tabby the Wild Cat

Dana Kubick

Piccadilly Press • London

When Tabby looks into the mirror
he doesn't see a small cat, he sees
himself as a big, brave, wild cat.

He doesn't see his home
as comfortable rooms,
but as a vast wilderness
full of adventure.

At night, Tabby dreams of hot sultry nights, sleeping under the moon and stars.

When morning light comes, Tabby is the first one to wake.

He goes out to patrol his territory and to walk in the tall grass.

He climbs to the very
top of the garden shed

. . . to watch over
his kingdom.

It's time to explore.
With big jumps, he leaps
from cliff to cliff.

When he gets thirsty,
Tabby drinks from majestic lakes.

He stalks his prey with silent steps.

He pounces.

But when he gets hungry,
it is nice to know . . .

. . . there is someone to
look after him.